The Mystery of the Silent Nightingale

*THE THREE COUSINS
DETECTIVE CLUB*

The Mystery of the Silent Nightingale

Elspeth Campbell Murphy
Illustrated by Joe Nordstrom

BETHANY HOUSE PUBLISHERS
MINNEAPOLIS, MINNESOTA 55438

Cover and internal illustrations by Joe Nordstrom

Published by Bethany House Publishers
A Ministry of Bethany Fellowship, Inc.
11300 Hampshire Avenue South
Minneapolis, Minnesota 55438

Printed in the United States of America

Library of Congress Cataloging-in-Publication Data

Murphy, Elspeth Campbell.
    The mystery of the silent nightingale / Elspeth Campbell
Murphy.
       p.   cm. — (The Three Cousins Detective Club ; 2)
    Summary: Sarah-Jane and her two cousins solve a mystery
involving an antique locket they plan to give their favorite baby-
sitter.
    [1. Mystery and detective stories. 2. Babysitters—Fiction.
3. Cousins—Fiction. 4. Christian life—Fiction.] I. Title.
II.Series: Murphy, Elspeth Campbell. Three Cousins Detective
Club ; 2.
PZ7.M95316Myhf   1994
[Fic]—dc20   94–16718
                                                  CIP
ISBN 1–55661–406–3   AC

In loving memory of my father-in-law,

Howard R. Murphy,

whose life was filled with
love, joy, peace,
patience, kindness, goodness,
faithfulness, gentleness, and self-control.

ELSPETH CAMPBELL MURPHY has been a familiar name in Christian publishing for over fifteen years, with more than seventy-five books to her credit and sales reaching five million worldwide. She is the author of the best-selling series *David and I Talk to God* and *The Kids From Apple Street Church*, as well as the 1990 Gold Medallion winner *Do You See Me, God?* A graduate of Trinity College and Moody Bible Institute, Elspeth and her husband, Mike, make their home in Chicago, where she writes full time.

Contents

1

In the Store Window

No one could spend more time looking in store windows than Sarah-Jane Cooper. At least that's what her cousins Timothy Dawson and Titus McKay thought. And now they said so. Loudly.

"Come *on*, S-J!" said Timothy. "We're supposed to meet Kelly at the library when she gets off work. We don't want to be late."

Titus added, "If we're late, we can't go over to the high school with Kelly to pick up her cap and gown."

But Sarah-Jane stood firm. "No, no. *Wait.* This is *about* Kelly.

She dragged the boys over to the crowded window of Mr. Robinson's antiques store. "I want to show you what I wish we could get Kelly for graduation. It's so cool!"

"I thought you already got Kelly's graduation present. It's supposed to be from all of us," said Timothy.

"Yes," said Titus. "I thought your mom let you pick Kelly's gift out of the catalog all by yourself."

No one could spend more time looking at catalogs than Sarah-Jane. At least that's what

Timothy and Titus thought.

But even they had to admit that Sarah-Jane had picked out the perfect gift for Kelly, who was going away to college. It was a beautiful wooden bookstand for holding a book open so you could study better. Kelly loved books. She was going to be either a teacher or a librarian.

Sarah-Jane gave an exasperated sigh. "I didn't say this thing I want to show you is what we're *going* to get Kelly. I said this thing is what I *wish* we could get her—if we hadn't already gotten her what we got her."

Titus looked at Timothy. "Are you following any of this?"

Timothy groaned and shook his head. Then he said to Sarah-Jane, "What's wrong with what we already got her?"

Sarah-Jane stared at the boys in alarm. "Nothing! I *love* what we got her! Why? Don't you?"

Timothy and Titus knew when they were licked. So they quit arguing and let Sarah-Jane drag them over to the store window.

And they had to admit that what Sarah-Jane wanted to show them was worth seeing.

"EXcellent," declared Titus.

"Neat-O," agreed Timothy.

2

The Silver Locket

They were looking at a beautiful silver locket that was almost a hundred years old. It was decorated with flowers around the edge. And right in the center there was a sweet little bird.

"It's a nightingale," said Sarah-Jane proudly. "Read the card beside it."

The card said that the nightingale was an early Christian symbol for joy. Mr. Robinson had explained it to Sarah-Jane, and now she explained it to Timothy and Titus.

Most birds went to sleep at nightfall. But the nightingale woke up in the early evening and sang through the night. The song of the nightingale was so sweet and happy sounding that it made people feel joyful and full of hope just to hear it.

This was true even when times were bad. And times were very bad for the early Christians. They were punished and even killed for believing in Jesus. They had to hide in underground cemetery tunnels. But even then they felt joy. They knew that no matter how bad things were, God was in charge. And that gave them hope.

To show how hopeful they felt, they drew pictures on the walls. They drew pictures of flowers and birds—nightingales.

Sarah-Jane said, "So ever since that time—almost two thousand years ago—the nightingale has been a Christian sign of joy."

3

The Best Baby-Sitter

*T*imothy said, "We have some cardinals in our backyard. But I don't think I've ever seen a nightingale."

"Or heard one, either," agreed Titus. "We have a lot of birds in the city. But mostly they're sparrows and pigeons."

Sarah-Jane shook her head. "That's because there are no nightingales in America. Mr. Robinson told me."

She sounded so sad the boys wanted to cheer her up.

"Well, at least you can see a picture of a nightingale on the locket," said Titus.

"Yes," said Timothy. "I'm glad you showed us the locket, S-J. It would have been a great thing to get for Kelly. That is, if we hadn't already gotten her what we got her."

"Which was also great," added Titus.

Sarah-Jane smiled. It was nice of her cousins to say so. But she wasn't sad because there were no nightingales nearby. (Although that *was* kind of sad when you stopped to think about it.) No, Sarah-Jane was sad because Kelly was going away.

Kelly Donovan had been Sarah-Jane's baby-sitter ever since Sarah-Jane could remember. When the boys came to visit—which was often—Kelly had been their baby-sitter, too.

As baby-sitters went, Kelly was pretty strict. But she was never mean. And you always had the feeling she knew what she was doing.

But best of all, Kelly always read to the cousins—even after they had learned to read for themselves. You never got too old to like hearing stories read aloud. The cousins especially liked mystery stories. They had a detective club. And they had even solved quite a few real mysteries themselves.

Kelly used to take Sarah-Jane, Titus, and Timothy to the library. In fact, she had been with them when Sarah-Jane got her first library card years ago.

And now Kelly was leaving. She wouldn't even be here for the summer. She was going away to attend special classes right after graduation.

Yes, things were changing. And Sarah-Jane didn't know how a person was supposed to feel joyful with all that change going on.

4

Seniors

*K*elly was just coming out of the library as the cousins hurried up.

"I hope we're not late," said Sarah-Jane.

"Nope, right on time," said Kelly with a smile. "This is fun having you guys come along."

The cousins chatted with Kelly all the way to the high school. But when they got there, they didn't say much. They were too busy looking around at the wide hallways and rows and rows of lockers. It seemed impossible to believe they would ever go to a school that big.

Or ever *be* as big as the seniors they saw all around them.

Kelly's friends were very nice to them. But Kelly was the nicest one of all. She even let them try on her cap. It was called a mortarboard.

"The tassel goes on the right-hand side of your face," Kelly explained. "Then, after you get your diploma, you move it to the left-hand side."

They each practiced a few times.

Sarah-Jane liked the mortarboard so much she hated to give it back. But she knew no one

would believe she was a senior no matter which side the tassel was on.

Of course, Kelly *was* a senior, and she was even more excited about the cap and gown than Sarah-Jane. (If that was possible.) She wanted to stop by her father's office to show him. So the cousins went along.

Mr. Donovan came out to the reception area to greet them. He looked so proud of Kelly, Sarah-Jane thought he was going to burst. Even Dorothy, the stern-looking office manager, smiled.

The cousins hung back by the door, feeling a little shy.

Then something strange happened.

5

Something Strange

A young woman came out of a back room and sat down at her desk. She glanced over at Kelly, Mr. Donovan, and Dorothy with a polite smile.

Then she saw the cousins.

Instantly her expression changed. Her eyes opened wide, and her mouth dropped open. Sarah-Jane didn't know when she had ever seen anyone look so surprised. But there was something else. It took Sarah-Jane a moment to figure it out. It was a look of pure joy.

The young woman looked back at Kelly as if she were seeing an angel. Kelly and her father were so busy talking they didn't notice. But when Dorothy turned around, the young woman turned bright pink. She snatched up some papers and turned away to the filing cabinets.

Sarah-Jane looked quickly at Timothy and Titus. She could tell by the way they looked back at her that they had noticed something, too.

"What was all that about?" muttered Timothy.

They stepped outside so they could talk better. They weren't sure why they didn't want to be overheard. It was just a feeling they had that something mysterious was going on.

Sarah-Jane said, "I don't get it. Why was that lady so surprised to see Kelly? She works for Kelly's dad. Kelly stops by the office a lot. They must have seen each other lots of times before."

Timothy added, "And if she was so glad to see Kelly, why didn't she say anything to her? Why did she just turn away like that?"

"But it wasn't just Kelly," said Titus. "It was *us*. I'm sure that lady recognized *us*."

"But how could she?" asked Sarah-Jane. "We've never seen her before in our lives."

6

Questions

When Kelly came out, the cousins were waiting for her—with questions. That's one thing detectives do. They ask questions.

Sarah-Jane said, "Kelly, who was that lady in there? Not Dorothy. The other one."

"That's Janice," said Kelly.

"Do you know her really well?" asked Titus.

"No," replied Kelly. "Hardly at all. I'm not even sure I know her last name. She's new. I've only seen her a few times. Why?"

"She looked like she recognized you," said Timothy.

Kelly gave a puzzled little laugh. "Well, of course she recognized me. She works for my dad."

"No," said Sarah-Jane. "We mean that she *really* recognized you. Like she knows you from somewhere."

"I don't see how," said Kelly. "Janice used to live in Fairfield. But my dad said she moved away about five years ago. She's only been back for a couple of months. Besides, if she knows me from somewhere, why hasn't she said anything?"

"That's just it," said Sarah-Jane. "It was like she just recognized you for the first time today. And how could that be when she's seen you before? And if she did, why not say something to you today?"

"Yes," said Timothy. "And it doesn't explain why it looked like she recognized *us* too."

"You, too?" asked Kelly. "But you don't know her, do you?"

The cousins shook their heads. They knew Kelly wouldn't ask them if they were imagining things. And she didn't. She knew they were detectives, who noticed what was going on around them. If Timothy, Titus, and Sarah-

Jane said they saw something strange, they saw something strange.

"I suppose we could just go back in and ask her," said Kelly doubtfully.

But the cousins knew that asking questions wasn't *always* the best thing to do. At least you had to pick the right time. Janice had been so flustered when Dorothy looked over at her. And now Dorothy was explaining something to Janice.

This was not the right time.

But the detective-cousins were still in the mood to ask questions. So after they dropped Kelly off, they went home and talked to Sarah-Jane's mother.

"Aunt Sue," began Titus. "Do you know a lady at Mr. Donovan's office named Janice?"

"I don't think so, Titus. Why?"

Timothy said, "Because when we stopped by there with Kelly, this lady—Janice—looked like she recognized us."

"*Really* recognized us," added Sarah-Jane. "Like we were special and she knew us from someplace."

"Did she say anything to you?" asked Sarah-Jane's mother.

"We don't think she had a chance to," said Sarah-Jane. "We think Dorothy scared her."

"Ah," said her mother. "That I can believe. I know Dorothy. She doesn't suffer fools gladly."

"What does *that* mean?" exclaimed Titus.

Aunt Sue laughed. "It means she doesn't have much patience with people. In this case, the word 'suffer' means to allow. Dorothy doesn't allow or put up with any foolishness. And that's all right, to a certain extent. But Dorothy carries it a little too far. She doesn't allow for any mistakes."

"We all make mistakes," said Timothy.

"That's right," said his aunt. "The point is to learn what we can from them and keep trying."

"So, if Dorothy is the office manager, that means she's Janice's boss, right?" asked Sarah-Jane.

"That's right," said her mother.

Titus said, "I can see why Janice looked so nervous."

7

Photographs

"Speaking of Janice—" said Sarah-Jane. "Kelly said Janice lived in Fairfield about five years ago. Maybe she knew us when we were little before she moved away."

"Yes, but five years ago we were only five years old," said Titus. "We would have looked really different then. Kelly would have looked really different, too."

Thinking about how they would have looked five years ago made the cousins want to get out the photograph albums.

Sarah-Jane's mother took a break from her work and sat down with them.

"Start from the beginning," said Sarah-Jane.

So they started with pictures of when they were newborn babies.

The cousins had all been born right about the same time. Sarah-Jane was the oldest. She was a month older than Timothy. Timothy was a month older than Titus.

Sarah-Jane came upon a picture of a young girl sitting on a couch, holding a baby. Sarah-Jane looked more closely.

"That's Kelly!" she exclaimed.

"That's right," said her mother. "And the baby is you. Kelly would have been about eight years old when you were born. She was too young to sit for you then. But she used to stop by after school to play with you. She used to love to read to you. When you got a little older—about the age your cousin Priscilla is now—you used to wait for Kelly. As soon as you saw her coming, you would grab a book. And you would yell, 'Weed tory! Weed tory!' "

In the old days when Timothy and Titus came to visit, Sarah-Jane's mother got out a special stroller she had found at a garage sale. It was made for triplets. When the cousins

rode in it, they looked like they were riding in a little train. And there was a picture of Kelly, proudly pushing them.

"You three were the cutest babies!" exclaimed Sarah-Jane's mother. "Everyone stopped to admire you. You didn't look that much alike. But everyone thought you were triplets until they found out you were actually cousins."

Later, of course, the cousins had gotten too big for the stroller.

When they were five and Kelly was thirteen, she had watched them by herself as her first baby-sitting job with all three of them. She had taken them to the library for story time. That had been an extra-special day for Sarah-Jane. She had learned to print her name well enough to get her very own library card. There was even a cute picture in the album of Kelly and the cousins when they came home that day. Sarah-Jane was holding the books she had checked out all by herself.

Timothy, Titus, and Sarah-Jane had a wonderful time looking at old pictures of themselves. It wasn't until they closed the photograph albums and put them away that they remembered something.

Janice.

There had been nothing in the albums to give them a clue as to who she was.

Yet the cousins were sure of two things:

Janice knew them.

And they didn't know her.

8

Another Mystery

*I*t was just after lunch that another mystery popped up.

Kelly called and asked the cousins to come over and help her look for something. Something, she said, that should be there—but wasn't.

Kelly lived only a couple of houses away from Sarah-Jane. The cousins hurried over. They found Kelly searching around the bushes in her front yard.

"What are you looking for?" asked Titus. "What did you lose?"

"I didn't exactly lose it," said Kelly. "I

never actually had it. See, someone left a graduation present on the porch. But there's no card to say who it's from. I'm thinking the card must have blown away. And I know you guys are great at finding things. . . ."

"Say no more," said Timothy.

"You've come to the right place," said Titus.

"Absolutely," said Sarah-Jane. Then she added, "There's not much wind today. It can't have blown far."

So they searched all around Kelly's house. Front yard. Backyard. Side of the house. Nothing.

They searched up and down the street. Across the street. And even all along the alley. Nothing.

"I feel terrible about this," said Kelly. "Someone went to all the trouble of getting me this *beautiful* graduation present that I just *love*. And now I can't even say thank you. How embarrassing! What is this person going to think?"

Sarah-Jane said, "It's possible the person just forgot to put the card on it. And so maybe that person will remember and tell you who the present was from."

"Unless . . ." said Timothy.

9

The Graduation Present

They all looked at Timothy, waiting for him to go on.

"Unless what?" asked Titus.

"Unless there never was a card in the first place," said Timothy. "Maybe whoever left the present doesn't want you to know who did it."

"You mean like a 'secret pal'?" asked Kelly.

"Sort of," said Timothy. "Sometimes the secret is just for fun. Or sometimes there's a good reason for someone—" He paused, trying to remember the right phrase. "Wishing to remain anonymous."

Titus said, "That happened to our grandfather once. Someone left a birthday present for him."

"Did he ever find out who left it?" Kelly asked.

The cousins looked at one another. They couldn't help smiling and feeling kind of pleased with themselves.

"We solved the mystery," said Sarah-Jane. "We found out who left the present, and why, and it all worked out fine."

"It sounds like you need the T.C.D.C.," said Titus.

Kelly's mother had just come out to see how it was going. She heard what Titus said, but she didn't understand it.

"What's a 'teesy-deesy'?" she asked.

"It's letters," explained Sarah-Jane. "Capital T. Capital C. Capital D. Capital C. It stands for the Three Cousins Detective Club."

Kelly sighed. "Well, I agree that I need detective help right now. I hate the thought of going away without knowing who gave me such a great present."

At the thought of Kelly going away, Sarah-Jane's stomach gave a little lurch. But all she said was, "Let's see what we can do. Why don't you show us the present. Maybe it will give us some idea of who left it."

It was a long shot, but the cousins knew they had to start somewhere.

Kelly led them inside. First she showed them the wrapping paper. It was decorated with rolled-up diplomas and mortarboards and words that said, *Congratulations, Graduate!*

"Nothing unusual here," said Titus. "You can buy this kind of paper just about anywhere this time of year."

They examined it carefully front and back for any kind of handmade notes or marks. There weren't any.

Then Kelly showed them the little box. Again, nothing unusual. It was when Kelly opened the box that the cousins gasped.

They were looking at a beautiful silver locket. It was decorated with flowers all around the edge. And right in the center there was a sweet little bird.

A nightingale.

10

Joy!

*T*imothy, Titus, and Sarah-Jane were too surprised to say a word.

"See? It's a locket," said Kelly, opening it up. She seemed surprised at how quiet the cousins were. "Nothing inside, of course. I thought there might be a clue in there. Maybe a picture of the person who sent it. But there wasn't. And there's nothing engraved on the back. But there is maybe *one* clue. See? This little information card tells about it. It tells how the nightingale is a Christian symbol for joy."

The cousins recognized the card as the one

from Mr. Robinson's store window. They leaned forward and read the card again.

Timothy said, "It looks like someone took a red pen and drew a circle around the word *joy*."

"And put an exclamation point beside it," added Titus.

"I noticed that," said Kelly. "What do you suppose it means? That graduation is a joyful time? I mean, I guess it is. But sometimes I don't feel so joyful about it."

Sarah-Jane looked up quickly.

Kelly must have guessed that Sarah-Jane wasn't feeling very joyful, either. She reached out and squeezed her hand.

"I'm sad about leaving home and all my friends. And—can I tell you a secret? I'm scared. Really scared about going away to college. I'm worried about finding my way around. And about fitting in. And about doing the work. But at the same time, I really want to go. I feel hopeful. And excited. Even though I'm sad and scared at the same time."

The cousins nodded. They knew what it was like to have all sorts of mixed-up feelings all at the same time. But it had never occurred

to them that seniors would be afraid of anything. Especially not Kelly.

"So, anyway," said Kelly. "I think this locket will help me. It will remind me that I can be hopeful no matter what's going on around me. Sarah-Jane, are you OK?"

Sarah-Jane forced herself to smile. "I'm fine," she said. But actually she felt very jealous. Who had sent 'her' present to 'her' Kelly? Sarah-Jane knew she wasn't being exactly fair. The locket was in the store window for anyone to buy. And Kelly wasn't just Sarah-Jane's friend. Sarah-Jane knew that. But she felt more than ever that she wanted to get to the bottom of this.

And she suddenly had an idea of how to do it.

11

At the Antiques Store

Sarah-Jane said, "We don't know who bought the locket. But we know where it came from because we saw it ourselves. It was in the window of Mr. Robinson's antiques store just this morning."

"It was?" exclaimed Kelly. "So that means someone bought it only a little while ago."

"Right," said Sarah-Jane. "So here's the plan: Mr. Robinson is a friend of ours. He likes to talk to the people who come in his store. So he must have talked to the person who bought the locket for you. We'll just go over there and ask him who it was."

Timothy and Titus stared at her as if to say, "Why didn't *we* think of that?"

But the detective-cousins had been around enough mysteries to know that things weren't always as simple as they seemed. Still, it was a good idea. So Timothy, Titus, and Sarah-Jane—plus Kelly—hurried off to the antiques store to get to the bottom of things.

But Mr. Robinson wasn't there.

"You just missed him," said his assistant, Bill. "He left on a buying trip. Won't be back for a couple of weeks."

Kelly groaned. "I'll be gone by then."

When she said that, Sarah-Jane's stomach gave another little lurch.

"Something I can help you with?" asked Bill.

"Maybe so," said Titus. "We're trying to find out who bought a silver locket today."

"Oh, right. The nightingale," Bill replied.

"Yes! Yes! Yes!" the cousins practically shouted together.

Bill took a step back, and that made them all laugh. Maybe they were getting a little carried away. It was just that they were so close to solving the mystery, they could hardly stand it.

Kelly took a deep breath and explained, "See—the locket was a graduation present for me. But I don't know who it's from. If there was a card, it got separated from the box. And now I don't know who to thank. So can you tell me who bought it?"

"I'm sorry. I can't help you there," said Bill.

12

More Questions

Kelly looked at Bill in dismay.

Timothy said, "Do you mean it was a secret? Did the person swear you to secrecy? Is that why you can't tell us?"

"No, nothing like that," said Bill. "I can't tell you who bought the locket because I don't know. I was working in the back room when this lady came in. Mr. Robinson waited on her."

A lady. Well, that narrowed it down.

A little. Not much. The cousins went into their questioning routine.

"So you never actually saw her at all?" asked Sarah-Jane.

"That's right," said Bill.

"And you didn't recognize her voice?" asked Timothy.

Bill shook his head.

"Well, what about the voice?" asked Titus. "Young? Old? Accent?"

"She wasn't a kid," said Bill. "And not an old lady. Somewhere in between. No accent."

The cousins glanced at one another.

This wasn't getting them very far.

Timothy had a sudden thought. "What about a credit card receipt? Could you get the name off of that?"

They all perked up until Bill shook his head apologetically. "Cash."

They had turned to leave when Sarah-Jane remembered the thing she knew about her friend Mr. Robinson. She remembered that he liked to chat with his customers.

She asked, "Did the lady and Mr. Robinson talk about anything?"

Bill frowned, thinking hard. The cousins could tell he was trying. He really was. But they knew not everyone noticed things as much as they did.

"They talked about the locket," said Bill slowly. "About how beautiful it was. About how the nightingale stood for joy. And Mr. Robinson asked her if she wanted a gift box. And she said yes, because it was a present. She said it was the perfect present, because it was for someone who had once brought her a lot of joy. Oh! And she said she had just run into that person today. This person had once helped her several years ago. She said the locket was her way of saying thank you all these years later."

Bill beamed at them, clearly pleased with himself.

"Well!" said Titus. "That certainly ties in with the little information card. I mean—the way the word *joy* had a circle around it and even an exclamation point."

"Now we're getting somewhere," said Timothy, sounding pretty joyful himself. "Who was it you helped so much, Kelly?"

But Kelly wasn't looking at all joyful. She looked flabbergasted. And she sounded as if she might start crying. "That's just it! I don't know! I don't *know*!"

Sarah-Jane didn't say anything for a moment. She was remembering the look of joy on someone's face. Joy when that person had looked at Kelly.

"Let's go," she said.

13

The T.C.D.C.

*J*anice was alone in the office when Kelly and the cousins came in. The time was right for asking some questions.

Janice looked startled—as if she knew that was what they had come for. Her eyes went right to the nightingale locket. Kelly had taken it out of her pocket and hung it around her neck.

Kelly said gently, "Janice, are you the person I should thank for this beautiful graduation present?"

At first Janice gave a little shake of her head. Then she turned pink and nodded.

"How did you know?" she asked softly.

Kelly said, "You have the T.C.D.C. to thank for that."

Janice looked confused. "What's a 'teesy-deesy'?" she asked.

"It's letters," explained Sarah-Jane for the second time that day.

"Capital T. Capital C. Capital D. Capital C. It stands for the Three Cousins Detective Club."

"Oh," said Janice, sounding as if that cleared things up a little. But only a little.

Timothy explained some more. "Well, see, it all started when S-J—Sarah-Jane—wanted to show us this neat-o present that she wished we could get Kelly for graduation."

"Oh, you guys!" interrupted Kelly, sounding again as if she was going to start crying. "I didn't know that! No wonder you were so quiet when I showed you the locket. Oh, you are just so sweet!"

She reached out and hugged Sarah-Jane, who happily hugged her back. Kelly would have hugged Timothy and Titus, too, but they were able to hop out of the way just in time.

"Anyway," said Titus. "We already had an

excellent present for Kelly, so we didn't think any more about it. But then the locket showed up with no name. And we knew it came from Mr. Robinson's store. So we went there to see who bought it. Only Mr. Robinson wasn't there. And all Bill could tell us was that it was a lady that Kelly helped once."

"But how did you know that was me?" asked Janice.

Sarah-Jane said, "Because of the way you looked at Kelly and us when we came in earlier today. It was like you recognized us. *Really* recognized us."

"You're exactly right," said Janice. "I *did* recognize you."

"But how?" asked Timothy. "We don't know you, do we?"

"And what did Kelly do to help you that made you remember her all these years?" asked Titus.

It had just occurred to the detective-cousins that they had come in to ask some questions. But so far all they had done was answer them.

It was time to hear from Janice.

14

The Nightingale's Story

*J*anice took a deep breath. "It all happened about five years ago. I—well, this is hard for me to admit. But, well, you see—I was all grown up before I learned how to read."

The cousins stared at her. They had never heard of such a thing. A grown-up who didn't know how to read? How could that be? They were too polite to say any of this. But Janice must have guessed what they were thinking. She said, "Oh, yes. There are lots of people like me. We try not to let anyone know. We're so embarrassed. We just sort of fake our way along. And it's not easy, believe me! In my case

I dropped out of school, which only made things worse.

"Then one day I overheard some people talking about special classes starting that afternoon at the library. The classes were for people like me. Grown-ups who had missed out somehow on learning to read, and who had to start at the beginning.

"I knew where the library was, so I got up my courage and went over there. But when I got there, I couldn't tell where the class was being held. And, of course, I couldn't read the signs. I couldn't ask the librarian, because there were some people I knew by her desk. I was just too embarrassed.

"I was all set to run out of there. But then I saw this young girl come in with three absolutely adorable children, two boys and a girl."

It took the cousins a moment to realize Janice was talking about them.

Janice smiled right at Sarah-Jane and said, "The little girl was getting her very own library card that day. And the look of joy on her face— well, you never saw anything like it! And I thought to myself, 'I want that, too. I want to learn how to read and check out books.'

56

"Well, the older girl—you, Kelly—was so good with the little ones that I thought, 'Here's someone I can trust.' I went up to you and asked if you could tell me where the class was. It was a moment that changed my life."

Kelly shook her head sadly. "I'm so sorry, Janice. I don't remember that."

But Janice just smiled. "It's all right. I think we all go through life, trying the best we can. And we don't always know the joy we bring to other people.

"Anyway, you told me to hold on a minute while you got the little ones settled in the story circle. Then you didn't just tell me where the class was. You went with me. And you said you could tell I was embarrassed about needing this class. But you said I shouldn't be. That it took courage to do what I was doing. And that I was doing the best thing in the world for myself.

"Well, you were right! I learned to read. And when I moved away I kept on studying until I got my diploma.

"I never forgot you, Kelly. But I just never made the connection between my boss's daughter and the young girl who helped me five years ago. You're all grown up now. It wasn't until you came in with those same three adorable kids—who are also pretty grown up—that I realized who you were! And then— well, I just wanted to get you something as a way of saying thank you. And the joy of the nightingale seemed just right."

"But this is *so cool!*." cried Sarah-Jane. "Why didn't you tell us before? Why did you want to keep the locket a secret?"

Janice looked down at her lap. "I guess you could call me a silent nightingale. I had all this joy, but I didn't want to sing out about it. To tell you the truth, not everyone is as understanding as you people are. I want so much to do a good job here. I just thought it might be harder if—if Dorothy found out I hadn't even learned to read until a few years ago."

Titus nodded. "Dorothy doesn't suffer fools gladly. Not that you're a fool," he added quickly. "I didn't mean that—"

Janice laughed. "I know exactly what you mean."

It was at that moment that the door opened and Mr. Donovan and Dorothy came in.

15

One More Mystery

Mr. Donovan looked pleased but surprised to see them. He said, "Back again? What's up? Kelly, where did you get that gorgeous locket?"

Kelly didn't lie. But she didn't give away Janice's secret. Rather she said, "It's a graduation present, Daddy. But, as Timothy once put it, the giver wishes to remain anonymous."

The cousins were impressed. But before anyone could reply, Janice spoke up. "It's all right, Kelly. You once told me I had nothing to be embarrassed about. And I think I need to remember that now."

Just as before, she took a deep breath. Quickly she repeated to Mr. Donovan what she had just told Kelly and the cousins.

It seemed to Sarah-Jane that if Mr. Donovan had been bursting with pride before, he was about to explode with pride now. He grinned at Kelly and said over and over, "That's my girl. That's my girl."

Even the cousins couldn't resist a little cheer when Janice got to the part about the three absolutely adorable children.

"So anyway," Janice finished. "I suddenly realized as I was telling Kelly about how she helped me that I want to help, too. I want to tutor people who don't know how to read. But how can I help them not be embarrassed—if I'm still embarrassed myself? Now, maybe if they know I did it, they'll believe they can do it, too."

"Humph!" said the gruff voice of Dorothy. Everyone jumped, even Mr. Donovan.

"If you want to tutor someone," she said, "how about starting with my grandson? He's having an awful time in school. I've tried to help him, goodness knows. But no, he doesn't want any help from Grandma Dorothy."

The cousins glanced at one another. They were too polite to say what they were thinking, which was: "Who would?"

But Kelly stepped in smoothly. "Well, sometimes it's easier to accept that kind of help from a stranger than from a relative."

Sarah-Jane didn't know when she had heard any kid sound so grown up. Not even a senior.

"Fair enough," replied Dorothy. "I'll pay for the lessons. I just want to help him. It doesn't matter how I do it. And I know Janice here is as smart as they come. Now, don't we all have work to do?"

With that she marched back to her desk, as though she was afraid she might say something else nice if she wasn't careful.

When the cousins got home later they got out the photograph albums again.

They especially wanted to see the picture of when they had come home from the library that day long ago. There was Sarah-Jane, with her arms full of books and her face full of joy.

When they got to the end of the album the

cousins saw something strange.

The most recent photograph was missing.

"Where's the picture of us?" cried Sarah-Jane.

"It's a mystery," answered her mother.

And that's all she would say.

But solving mysteries was what the cousins did for fun.

"Let's think this through," said Titus. "You take a picture out of the album. Where do you put it?"

"In a picture frame?" suggested Timothy. "In a wallet?"

Sarah-Jane gasped. You would have to cut the picture down to get it to fit, of course. But—yes!—there was one other place she could think of where you could put a photograph.

And she was right.

That evening after graduation she asked Kelly if she could see inside the locket.

Kelly laughed and said, "You three don't miss much, do you? I didn't think it would take you long to figure it out. See? The nightingale on the outside will remind me of the joy I was able to bring to Janice. And the pictures on the

inside will remind me of some people who have brought a whole lot of joy to me."

She opened the locket and showed them. On the one side there was a picture of Timothy and Titus together. On the other side there was a picture of Sarah-Jane.

Kelly reached out and caught Sarah-Jane in a big, happy hug.

Timothy and Titus tried to hop out of the way.

They didn't make it.

The End